A PUPPET TREASURE BOOK
Nursery Rhymes

A PUPPET TREASURE BOOK
Nursery Rhymes

Pictures by Tadasu Izawa and Shigemi Hijikata

Publishers · GROSSET & DUNLAP · New York

Contents

Library of Congress Catalog Card Number: 76-158759
ISBN : 0-448-12288-X

Illustrations Copyright © 1968, 1969, 1971, 1977 by Tadasu Izawa and Shigemi Hijikata
through management of Dairisha, Inc. Printed and bound in Japan
by Zokeisha Publications, Ltd., Roppongi, Minato-ku, Tokyo.
1985 Printing

A Child's Garden of Verses

By Robert Louis Stevenson

The Swing

How do you like to go up in a swing,
   Up in the air so blue?
Oh, I do think it the pleasantest thing
   Ever a child can do!

Up in the air and over the wall,
   Till I can see so wide,
Rivers and trees and cattle and all
   Over the countryside—

Till I look down on the garden green,
   Down on the roof so brown—
Up in the air I go flying again,
   Up in the air and down!

My Ship and I

O it's I that am the captain of a tidy little ship,
  Of a ship that goes a-sailing on the pond;
And my ship it keeps a-turning all around and all about;
But when I'm a little older, I shall find the secret out—
  How to send my vessel sailing on beyond.

At the Seaside

When I was down beside the sea
A wooden spade they gave to me
To dig the sandy shore.

My holes were empty like a cup.
In every hole the sea came up,
Till it could come no more.

Rain

The rain is raining all around,
It falls on field and tree,
It rains on the umbrellas here
And on the ships at sea.

Block City

What are you able to build with your blocks?
Castles and palaces, temples and docks.
Rain may keep raining, and others go roam,
But I can be happy and building at home.

Singing

Of speckled eggs the birdie sings
 And nests among the trees;
The sailor sings of ropes and things
 In ships upon the seas.

The children sing in far Japan,
 The children sing in Spain;
The organ with the organ man
 Is singing in the rain.

Where Go the Boats

Dark brown is the river,
Golden is the sand.
It flows along forever,
With trees on either hand.

Green leaves a-floating,
Castles of the foam,
Boats of mine a-boating—
Where will all come home?

On goes the river
And out past the mill,
Away down the valley,
Away down the hill.

Away down the river,
A hundred miles or more,
Other little children
Shall bring my boats ashore.

Whole Duty of Children

A child should always say what's true
And speak when he is spoken to,
And behave mannerly at table;
At least, as far as he is able.

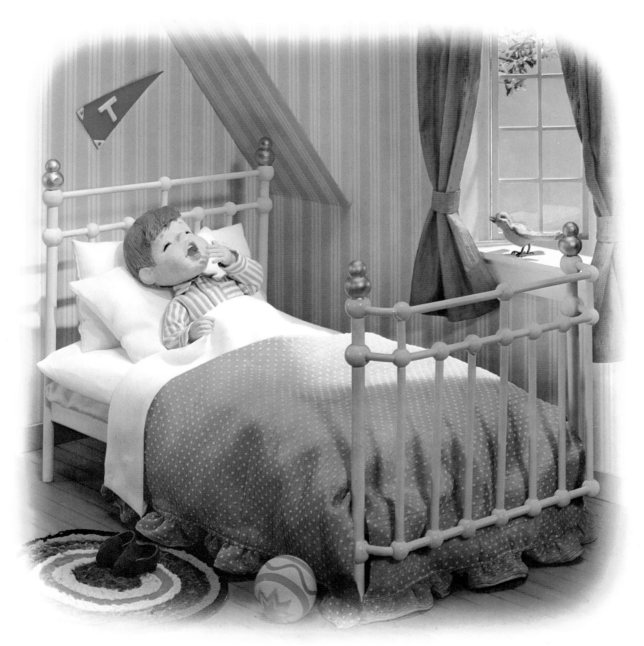

Time to Rise

A birdie with a yellow bill
Hopped upon my windowsill,
Cocked his shining eye and said:
"Ain't you 'shamed, you sleepyhead!"

17

Bed in Summer

In winter I get up at night
And dress by yellow candlelight.
In summer, quite the other way,
I have to go to bed by day.

I have to go to bed and see
The birds still hopping on the tree
Or hear the grown-up people's feet
Still going past me in the street.

And does it not seem hard to you,
When all the sky is clear and blue,
And I should like so much to play,
To have to go to bed by day?

19

Counting Rhyme

Ten little Indians
   standing in a line;
One went home
   and then there were nine.

Nine little Indians
    swinging on a gate;
One jumped off
    and then there were eight.

Eight little Indians
    went to the town of Devon;
One said he'd stay there
    and then there were seven.

Seven little Indians
    playing funny tricks;
One went to ride
    and then there were six.

Six little Indians
    learning how to dive;
One swam away
    and then there were five.

Five little Indians
  peeped through the door;
One ran behind
  and then there were four.

Four little Indians
    climbed up a tree;
One slid down
    and then there were three.

Three little Indians
    out in a canoe;
One hopped out on shore
    and then there were two.

Two little Indians
    playing in the sun;
One fell asleep
    and then there was one.

One little Indian
    playing all alone;
He went in the house
    and then there was none.

Mother Goose

Little Boy Blue

Little Boy Blue, come blow your horn!
The sheep's in the meadow, the cow's in the corn.

Where is the little boy who looks after the sheep?
He's under the haystack, fast asleep.
Will you wake him? No, not I!
For if I do, he's sure to cry.

Peter, Peter

Peter, Peter, pumpkin-eater,
Had a wife and couldn't keep her;
He put her in a pumpkin shell,
And there he kept her very well.

Humpty Dumpty

Humpty Dumpty sat on a wall,
Humpty Dumpty had a great fall;
All the King's horses and all the King's men
Couldn't put Humpty together again.

Old King Cole

Old King Cole
Was a merry old soul,
And a merry old soul was he;
He called for his pipe
And he called for his bowl,
And he called for his fiddlers three.

Every fiddler
Had a fiddle,
And a very fine fiddle had he;
Oh, there's none so rare
As can compare
With King Cole and his fiddlers three.

Jack, Be Nimble

Jack, be nimble,
Jack, be quick,
Jack, jump over the candlestick.

Rock-a-Bye, Baby

Rock-a-bye, baby, on the tree top;
When the wind blows, the cradle will rock;
When the bough breaks, the cradle will fall;
Down will come baby, cradle and all.

Little Miss Muffet

Little Miss Muffet sat on a tuffet,
Eating her curds and whey;
There came a big spider,
Who sat down beside her,
And frightened Miss Muffet away!

Baa, Baa, Black Sheep

Baa, baa, black sheep, have you any wool?
Yes, sir, yes, sir — three bags full;
One for my master, one for my dame,
And one for the little boy who lives in our lane.

Mary's Lamb

Mary had a little lamb,
Its fleece was white as snow;
And everywhere that Mary went,
The lamb was sure to go.

Twinkle, Twinkle

Twinkle, twinkle, little star,
How I wonder what you are!
Up above the world so high,
Like a diamond in the sky.

Hickory, Dickory, Dock!

Hickory, dickory, dock!
The mouse ran up the clock;
The clock struck one,
The mouse ran down,
Hickory, dickory, dock!

The Three Little Kittens

Three little kittens
They lost their mittens,
   And they began to cry,
"Oh, Mother dear,
We sadly fear
   That we have lost our mittens."

"What, lost your mittens!
You naughty kittens!
    Then you shall have no pie."
Mee-ow, mee-ow, mee-ow.
No, you shall have no pie.

The three little kittens
They found their mittens,
   And they began to cry,
"Oh, Mother dear,
See here, see here,
   For we have found our mittens."

"Put on your mittens,
You silly kittens,
    And you shall have some pie."
    Purr-r, purr-r, purr-r,
    Oh, let us have some pie.

The three little kittens
Put on their mittens
    And soon ate up the pie;

"Oh, Mother dear,
We greatly fear
  That we have soiled our mittens."
"What, soiled your mittens!
You naughty kittens!"
  Then they began to sigh.
  Mee-ow, mee-ow, mee-ow.
  Then they began to sigh.

The three little kittens
They washed their mittens,
  And hung them out to dry;

"Oh, Mother dear,
Do you not hear
    That we have washed our mittens?"
"What, washed your mittens!
Then you're good kittens,
    But I smell a rat close by."
    Mee-ow, mee-ow, mee-ow.
    We smell a rat close by.

The House That Jack Built

This is the house that Jack built.

This is the malt
That lay in the house
  that Jack built.

This is the rat,
That ate the malt
That lay in the house
  that Jack built.

This is the cat,
That killed the rat,
That ate the malt
That lay in the house
    that Jack built.

This is the dog,
That worried the cat,
That killed the rat,
That ate the malt
That lay in the house
    that Jack built.

This is the cow
    with the crumpled horn,
That tossed the dog,
That worried the cat,
That killed the rat,
That ate the malt
That lay in the house
    that Jack built.

This is the maiden
  all forlorn,
That milked the cow
  with the crumpled horn,
That tossed the dog,

That worried the cat,
That killed the rat,
That ate the malt
That lay in the house
  that Jack built.

This is the man
  all tattered and torn,
That kissed the maiden
  all forlorn,
That milked the cow
  with the crumpled horn
That tossed the dog,
That worried the cat,
That killed the rat,
That ate the malt
That lay in the house
  that Jack built.

This is the priest
   all shaven and shorn,
That married the man
   all tattered and torn,
That kissed the maiden
   all forlorn,
That milked the cow
   with the crumpled horn,
That tossed the dog,
That worried the cat,
That killed the rat,
That ate the malt
That lay in the house
   that Jack built.

This is the cock
    that crowed in the morn,
That waked the priest
    all shaven and shorn,
That married the man
    all tattered and torn,
That kissed the maiden
    all forlorn,
That milked the cow
    with the crumpled horn,
That tossed the dog,
That worried the cat,
That killed the rat,
That ate the malt
That lay in the house
    that Jack built.

This is the farmer
    sowing his corn,
That kept the cock
    that crowed in the morn,
That waked the priest
    all shaven and shorn,
That married the man
    all tattered and torn,
That kissed the maiden
    all forlorn,
That milked the cow
    with the crumpled horn,
That tossed the dog,
That worried the cat,
That killed the rat,
That ate the malt
That lay in the house
    that Jack built.

This is the horse
    and the hound and the horn,
That belonged to the farmer
    sowing his corn,
That kept the cock
    that crowed in the morn,
That waked the priest
    all shaven and shorn,
That married the man
    all tattered and torn,
That kissed the maiden
    all forlorn,
That milked the cow
    with the crumpled horn,
That tossed the dog,
That worried the cat,
That killed the rat,
That ate the malt
That lay in the house
    that Jack built.

Little Nursery Rhymes

Little Tom Tucker
    Sings for his supper.
What shall we give him?
    White bread and butter.
How shall he cut it
    Without any knife?
How shall he marry
    Without any wife?

Bow-wow-wow!
    Whose dog art thou?
Little Tom Tucker's dog,
    Bow-wow-wow!

This little pig went to market;

This little pig stayed home;

This little pig had roast beef;

This little pig had none;

This little pig cried, "Wee-wee-wee!"

All the way home.

Jumping Joan

Here am I,
Little jumping Joan;
When nobody's with me,
I'm always alone.

Jack Horner

Little Jack Horner
Sat in the corner,
Eating his Christmas pie;
He put in his thumb
And pulled out a plum,
And said, "What a good boy am I!"

Little Boys and Little Girls

What are little girls made of?
What are little girls made of?
Sugar and spice, and all that's nice;
That's what little girls are made of.

What are little boys made of?
What are little boys made of?
Frogs and snails, and puppy dogs' tails;
That's what little boys are made of.

Little Bo-Peep

Little Bo-Peep has lost her sheep,
And can't tell where to find them;
Leave them alone, and they'll come home,
And bring their tails behind them.

Little Robin Redbreast

Little Robin Redbreast
Sat upon a rail;
Niddle-naddle went his head,
Wiggle-waggle went his tail.

Wee Willie Winkie

Wee Willie Winkie runs through the town,
Upstairs and downstairs, in his nightgown,
Rapping at the window, crying through the lock,
"Are the children in their beds? . . .
Now it's eight o'clock."

Polly Flinders

Little Polly Flinders
Sat among the cinders
Warming her pretty little toes;
Her mother came and caught her,
And spanked her little daughter
For spoiling her nice new clothes.

Here We Go Round the Mulberry Bush

Here we go round the mulberry bush,
The mulberry bush, the mulberry bush,
Here we go round the mulberry bush,
So early in the morning.

This is the way we wash the clothes,
Wash the clothes, wash the clothes,
This is the way we wash the clothes,
So early Monday morning.

This is the way we iron the clothes,
Iron the clothes, iron the clothes,
This is the way we iron the clothes,
So early Tuesday morning.

This is the way we mend the clothes,
Mend the clothes, mend the clothes,
This is the way we mend the clothes,
So early Wednesday morning.

This is the way we sweep the floor,
Sweep the floor, sweep the floor,
This is the way we sweep the floor,
So early Thursday morning.

This is the way we scrub the floor,
Scrub the floor, scrub the floor,
This is the way we scrub the floor,
So early Friday morning.

This is the way we bake the bread,
Bake the bread, bake the bread,
This is the way we bake the bread,
So early Saturday morning.

This is the way we go to church,
Go to church, go to church,
This is the way we go to church,
So early Sunday morning.

JU